STOV ✓

THE BOY WITH THE PARROT

By ELIZABETH COATSWORTH

THE CAT AND THE CAPTAIN

TOUTOU IN BONDAGE

THE SUN'S DIARY

THE BOY WITH THE PARROT

THE CAT WHO WENT TO HEAVEN

(Preparing)

With other publishers, books of verse:

FOX FOOTPRINTS

BEYOND ATLAS

COMPASS ROSE

The ambassadors drew two pictures.

THE BOY
WITH THE
PARROT

A Story of Guatemala

By ELIZABETH COATSWORTH

PICTURES BY
WILFRID S. BRONSON

NEW YORK
THE MACMILLAN COMPANY
1939

PRINTED IN THE UNITED STATES OF AMERICA
AMERICAN BOOK—STRATFORD PRESS, INC., NEW YORK

This Book is
Gratefully and Affectionately
Dedicated to
MORTON SMITH
Advisor-in-Chief
of Every Expedition

CONTENTS

ILLUSTRATIONS

THE BOY WITH THE PARROT

I: STARTING OFF

SEBASTIAN was setting forth into the world. He couldn't have told you whether he was glad or sorry. He was proud of the pack that hung so heavily from the leather strap across his forehead, he was proud of his sandals which he had made himself, and of his new straw hat. He was proud of the carrier's stick he carried in his hand, and of the blue enamel cup that hung from the network of the cacaste frame holding his load. He hoped all the neighbors would notice him starting off.

But he was frightened, too, and lonely already, only fifty steps from his own door. He turned round again.

"Keep a brave heart!" called his mother, waving her hand, "and remember your manners, your prayers, and your poor widowed mother."

"I'll remember!" he shouted back and broke into a trot, picking his way among the blocks of lava along the path. The village of San Lucas Toliman was built on an old lava flow that had once poured into the blue waters of the lake below. In the rough crevasses the houses huddled, made of sticks wattled together, daubed with mud, their thatches ending in ridgepoles of broken pots to shed the rain. Sebastian never guessed it was a poor village. He thought the old white Spanish church with its two bearded lemon-colored lions above the door the finest in all Guatemala. As he passed, he paused and bent one knee to all the saints whom he knew were inside, Christ the baby in a lace cap, and the sad Christ carrying a cross with gold leaves about it, and the Virgin Mary in a blue velvet dress with a real lace handkerchief and a watch on her wrist, and Saint Luke, and all the others.

The priest had taught him Spanish, and that was fortunate his mother said, for he would meet many, many people who would not understand the Indian speech of his village.

Sebastian knew that the steamer was in. Already people who had been at the great market at Sololá were climbing the path toward him. He saw a neighbor with a fine turkey tied comfortably in a net on top of the cacaste. The turkey looked down at Sebastian like a cross old man as they passed. Then came a barefooted woman with a little pig in a harness running in front of her like a dog. But the climb tired its short fat legs, and Sebastian saw her stoop and pick it up, squealing like mad, to carry under one arm.

At the corner the view of the lake burst on him as he had seen it every day of his life. But now *he* was going to see what lay on the further shore, *he* was going to Sololá and Tecpan, and further still, even to the capital itself. His heart beat so fast it almost choked him.

"Look out!" called a man's voice. Sebastian, full of his thoughts, had almost walked into a mule's heels. "I don't want a big thing like you pushing the poor beast into the water," the man went on, while several people laughed.

"He'd be the better for a bath," said Sebas-

tian sturdily, determined not to be made fun of in his own town.

"The little flea will jump far," said the man good-naturedly. He had a long whip of braided rawhide in his hand, fastened to a loop that had his name, Rodrigo, written on it in red wool. He was in charge of ten mules carrying sugar in big black balls wrapped in dry leaves which were to be loaded on the steamer. The mules were making themselves comfortable after their trip, pawing in the dust and chewing at the bushes near them.

When Sebastian reached the steamer the

[4]

gangplank was being used. Men were trying
to load some steers, and the steers didn't want
to be loaded. The leader, a big tan creature,
stood in the middle of the planks, his four hoofs
bunched together, pulling back so hard that he
was almost sitting on his tail, while two men
hauled at a rope about his horns and two more
shoved him from behind and all four yelled.

"The worse they scare him, the heavier he'll
be," thought Sebastian, and after a minute,
when the men stopped to catch their breaths, he
said to one of them:

"Excuse me, sir, but my mother says a blind
man will walk on a ridgepole."

[5]

"Huh?" said the man and scratched his head. "Well, it's worth trying." And he tied a cloth over the steer's eyes. Not seeing the water through the cracks, the creature walked quietly aboard and allowed himself to be tied to a post near the prow of the boat. Sebastian paid his fare and followed, feeling a little as the steer had felt.

All about him people were crowded, sitting on the deck, their bundles beside them. He crouched down until the bottom of his cacaste touched, then slipped his forehead from the leather band. His neck was strong, but the load was a man's load and heavy for him. It seemed good to be able to stand up and stretch. Now he looked at the shore. Women he knew were drawing water in the big two-handled jars of his village, setting them when full on their heads and climbing the steep hill toward their houses, their arms swinging quietly at their sides. The new wife of a neighbor was washing her hair, knee-deep in the lake, while a buzzard perching on a rock near by watched her patiently, hoping she might be careless enough to lay down,

[6]

even for a moment, the ball of black soap she was using. Then it would be gobble soap, and fly away buzzard.

A deckhand blew a horn. Somewhere in the village above, Sebastian knew his mother was waiting to hear that sound. In a moment now they would be off. A last passenger or two tore down the bank and across the gangplank, the engines began to throb, and the little vessel stirred under Sebastian's sandals. Someone on the shore cast loose the ropes, and the boat pushed itself backward, swung and, gathering speed, headed into the lake. Sebastian's adventures had begun.

II: THE PACK

THE lake's name was Atitlan. It was miles long and very clear and bright, and there were volcanoes and mountains like a wall in a circle about it. From the mountains rose pillars of smoke where the men were beginning to burn over new land at the end of the dry season to plant their cornfields. The slopes were very steep, and the heavy smoke rose and mingled with the clouds. Sebastian could see them all reflected in the water below him, mountains, smoke and clouds and his own brown face looking up at him from wide black eyes.

"You'll be drowned," he warned his reflection half in earnest. "Don't you know that the lake is full of whirlpools to swallow up swimmers? Come back, I say!" And he pulled back his head, for he hated to have any part of him sliding there like a lizard in the shadow of the boat.

[8]

No one talked to him, being busy about their own affairs. He could have spoken to someone if he had wanted to, but he was full of his thoughts. In the pack beside him lay all his mother's earnings. Here an egg and there a chicken, with a little fruit one morning and a few bunches of onions the next—so in the dusty marketplace the money had been gathered which two days ago had bought the peddler's pack. Only last week the man had come to town, gaunt with fever, sometimes burning hot and sometimes shaking with cold. His strength was almost gone. He needed weeks in their high mountains to shake off this lowland sickness. Meantime he must sell his wares.

Sebastian's mother was a woman of determination. She looked at Sebastian. He was young, he was small, but it was a bright and knowing eye that looked back at her. She would chance it. Such an opportunity might never come again.

So she took the money she had saved and went

to the house where lay the sick man. For hours they haggled. He was a peddler and she was a market woman and they each knew every trick of the game. Finally she took the necklace of old coins and red beads from her neck and, flinging it on the small pile of money before her, held out open palms to say that she had nothing more. And as by that time the peddler was growing tired, the bargain was made.

Sebastian would never forget his first look at the treasure. There were little mirrors with pink celluloid backs, and combs for women's hair, in all colors, set with brilliants. There were rolls of foreign ribbons, and cotton flowers. There were necklaces of gold and silver glass beads, and long glass earrings that tinkled against each other. There were celluloid dolls with blue eyes, and rattles, and for men ties and penknives and brass rings dipped in gold. There were scissors and thread and needles in neat packages, tin whistles, and a dozen things beside. Sebastian had never seen such wonders. He covered his eyes with his hands, but when he looked again his mother had spread out bolts of cerise and scarlet and turquoise and electric blue silk for

[10]

scarves, and dimity for dresses, such as she said the women wore in the big towns. She spread a cloth on the floor, and they knelt, laying out one beautiful thing after another, touching each one and laughing for pleasure.

But after a while, his mother turned serious.

"It is a large lump of sugar for a small bee," she exclaimed, sitting back on her bare heels and frowning. Sebastian suddenly looked very little to her, and she had heard that there was much wickedness in the world beyond San Lucas Toliman. Suppose he should be foolish, or that someone should rob him? Perhaps, after all, it had not been wise to buy the peddler's pack.

But "No! no!" cried Sebastian, in love with the things spread before them; and in a panic for fear his mother might change her mind, "I'll wear a big hat, mother, and no one will see how small I am, and I'll carry my knife, and if anyone bothers me they'll find I have a long sting!"

So his mother between laughter and tears said he might go. How can a widow with only one child know what is best to do? If he remained at home, who knows that a mad dog might not bite him?

But when Sebastian stepped off on a strange shore that noon, he didn't feel as brave as he had felt the night before at home. Yet he shifted his heavy cacaste on its strap, took his staff in a firm hand, and followed the other Indians along a steep uphill road. Once only he turned to look back. Below him lay the bright blue waters of Atitlan in a wall of mountains that seemed scarcely less blue, and far away at the end of the lake he saw, no bigger than his thumbnail, San Lucas Toliman, where he had eaten his breakfast that morning.

NO BIGGER THAN HIS THUMBNAIL

III: THE GYPSIES

IT WAS early dusk when Sebastian reached Sololá. All the houses were covered with plaster painted terra cotta, blue, or lavender, with bars of wrought iron across the windows. The streets were paved with cobbles. He was pleased to see, however, that, great as the market square was—and he had never dreamed there could be such a big one—the church was smaller than the church of San Lucas Toliman and had no yellow lions. That gave him confidence to make his way through the crowds. Many people were leaving the market, others were packing up their wares, and some had already built cooking fires beside the streets. He saw crowds in front of open booths where soups were bubbling in round jars of pottery, and a dazzling array of the meat of dry fish, turtles, alligators, or lizards was offered, while turkeys and chickens, tethered each by one leg, pecked for crumbs among the patrons' feet.

Sebastian sniffed greedily. He was hungry and tired. The load on his back had grown heavier with every uphill mile, and now it seemed ready to crush him. But the boat fare

[14]

had used up what little money he had. His pack must make his fortune, and for to-night he would have to be satisfied with the flat corn meal tortillas his mother had made him, already clammy and tasteless.

He was passing by an open piece of land with a stake fence and a gate, when he saw a woman walking toward him from a street fountain. She was taller than anyone he had ever seen before, man or woman, and she moved as though her feet slid over the ground, though when she came nearer he saw that she wore shoes very old and run over at the heels. Her skirt was of red cotton, and her sacque white and flounced, and both swayed about her as she walked, one hand on the big copper water jar on her head, while the other held a second jar. The copper shone like gold in the sunset. She was smoking a cigarette and looking at no one. The market and its Indians did not seem to be there. She was from another world and, unlike any girl of Sebastian's people, she wore a rose in her hair. He stopped, as much astonished as if he had seen one of the saints in the church at San Lucas Toliman climb down from its shrine. He had expected to see strange sights. Now he was seeing them. But as the tall woman drew near the bars, he suddenly thought of his mother's parting words and remembered his manners.

"With your permission," he murmured and swung open the gate for her to pass with the heavy load of water she carried so casually.

"May God reward you," she said formally. Then her gray eyes rested on his tired face and she stopped, raised her free hand to her cigarette, took a deep puff, and went on in a singsong voice:

"Where are you off to, all by your young lone?"

"I'm a peddler," Sebastian answered proudly, trying to stand straight, but the cacaste on his back was too heavy.

"Come with me, peddler," said the woman and swung off down a path, never glancing behind her to see whether or not he was following. He hesitated. Was it safe to go with a stranger away from the square, a woman of some giant race he had never even heard of? He thought that his mother would have said no, but he found himself trotting after her through the field.

[16]

In a few minutes they had reached two tents behind which mules were picketed. At a fire another tall woman with a bright scarf over her hair was cooking, while an almost naked child, wearing a string of cloudy yellow beads, was playing with a puppy. An old man in khaki clothes and a wide slouch hat was sitting in the doorway of one of the tents, and two younger men were feeding the mules with dried corn stalks.

"I have brought a peddler home for supper," said the woman with the rose in her hair.

"He is welcome," answered the old man, raising a thin face and smiling a little. No Indian ever had such a long white beard. Soon the men, including Sebastian, were given plates heaped with stew from the black kettle, and the women ate when they were through.

"So you are a trader?" asked one of the young men when the meal was over, standing looking down at Sebastian with his thumbs stuck in his wide belt.

"A bird is known by its bill," answered Sebastian, pointing to his pack. He was afraid perhaps he was not being taken seriously enough.

[17]

"A fine life is trading, my son," said the old man. "I've traded all my life, mules and horses, horses and mules. I can tell you the age and condition of an animal as far off as I can hear the sound of his hoofs on the road. And I know buyers too. And I can tell if rain is coming by the stars. Though in this land of rainy and dry seasons, small good it does to be a weather forecaster," he added, sighing.

Sebastian had to stretch his ears to understand all the old man said, for like the woman he spoke with a curious accent.

"I suppose," suggested Sebastian, "you must have traveled far, perhaps even further than Guatemala City."

"Yes, even further," said the old man. "We spent six weeks crossing the ocean, for one thing."

Sebastian had heard of the ocean but did not know it was so large.

"What did you eat?" he asked, "and how could a ship travel so far without rest?" And he thought of the two hours on Lake Atitlan which had seemed to him such a journey that morning.

They explained, and told him about their own

country which was called Hungary, though they were called gypsies. He could not imagine the things they pictured, but saw a highway stretching to a lake greater than Atitlan with shores crowded with many beautiful giants cooking stews in iron pots, while the firelight flickered along the canvas of their tents.

At last they gave him a saddle to sleep on and a blanket, and no sooner had he fitted his head in the hollow of the saddle than he was asleep, and was being wakened for breakfast in the half light before dawn. When they had eaten, the girl for whom he had opened the gate asked to see his things and bought a pair of gold glass earrings, while the others filled his heart with pride by admiring everything. When he had packed again they strolled with him to the square in the cool early morning light.

"Farewell, farewell," said the old man while Sebastian kissed his hand respectfully, "and now let me give you a word of advice as an old peddler to a young one. No matter what pillow you're offered, sleep with your head on your pack."

Sebastian thanked him again. But what he

never guessed, as he trotted out of Sololá, was that the gypsies had gone through his wares during the night while he slept so soundly. It was his friend who had insisted that everything should be put back again in its place.

"Our food is in him, and our blanket over him," she said angrily when the others protested. "I didn't bring the little Indian back to be robbed." And finally the old man had upheld her.

IV: IN THE HIGHLANDS

THE gypsies had told Sebastian that if he traveled well he could be over the mountains and into Tecpan by night.

"There is no one on the road to whom you could sell a bent nail," they said. "The mountains! they are full of cold fogs and cliffs, not market squares. But Tecpan is a different matter. It is an old town and a large one."

So he swung his stick bravely and broke into the carrier's shuffling trot that wears down the miles. There were many others already on the road, carriers too, often in groups of five or six from one village. A glance at their clothes told where they came from. Some of the men wore shirts with red sleeves, and short trousers of red

and white hand-woven cotton; some had spots of embroidery on their trousers; some wore gray and white woolen tartans round their hips; and there were others that looked fine as village mayors in coats and trousers of dark blue embroidered with lavender suns at the neck and knees.

Most of them carried a cacaste like his own, showing above their shoulders, and a wide straw hat wound with a band of red cloth tilted up by the leather strap across their foreheads. If the loads were heavy, the men went bent over so far that Sebastian could see little but their chins unless they looked up in passing. Sometimes they spoke to him, and sometimes they trotted by without a word.

Sebastian looked carefully to see what they were carrying. In both directions towering loads of glazed jars and plates were going past, for each village made its own design and sold the pottery throughout the country. Coming toward

him there seemed to be livestock and fresh vege-
tables and dried meats and wool blankets from
the sheep country for the market at Sololá;
while going in his direction were loads of
onions, white as pearls, and the black balls of
crude sugar he had seen being loaded on the
steamer at San Lucas Toliman. He looked
eagerly to see if anyone seemed to be carrying
foreign goods like his, but he happened to see
no one.

Sometimes he passed women, walking straight
as trees, their babies slung on their backs and
their burdens carried on their heads. They
never used their hands to steady them, but
trotted demurely in and out among the stones of
the road, their tight bright skirts catching their
knees at every step, their bodices gay with
designs in scarlet, indigo, or lavender, often of
beasts or birds with square wings. Usually they
carried a scarlet cloth on their heads to soften
the weight of their loads, and underneath it one

could see their black hair, twisted about their heads with red or purple wool. They always had a word to call to Sebastian, and several times, in spite of what the gypsies had said, a group would ask him to stop and show them his wares. Then he laid a cloth by the road and brought out his treasures, and twice some woman bought a chain of gold glass beads, for in this part of the country they loved to wear them in ropes three inches thick about their necks.

As the sun climbed toward noon Sebastian's road grew steeper and steeper, and he left the fields behind and entered into the forests. Now he met few carriers. Often he saw no one for several miles, and then he might hear a driver yelling at his mules, or catch far ahead the thin blare of a horn where a convoy of ox-carts slowly toiled up the ravines, each driver walking at the head of his team, directing them with a long stick.

How Sebastian wished people would buy heavy things! The pack felt no better for having a pair of earrings and some glass necklaces gone. He stopped, eased his load from the headband, and poured a drink of water into his blue cup

[24]

from a small gourd with a stopper that hung beside it. But before drinking, he put a handful of meal in it, making a mixture that would serve both as food and drink.

Then he shouldered his pack again and climbed on. He needed his strength, for now he was traveling at the edge of a precipice. A cold white mist swept over the mountain tops. He could see only the nearer trees, great pines of some sort, shaggy with moss, and with orchids starring the crotches of their branches. The world as he had known it was wiped out. Now he had nothing but his highway unrolling under his feet. He felt terribly alone. He wondered what the people were doing in San Lucas Toliman.

But still he climbed. And after a while he heard the sound of water falling down the mountain side. He hurried toward it and suddenly, out of the mists, he made out a tall tree beside the road and a trickle of stream near by it, dammed into a small pool, and, leaning against the trunk, a peddler of parrots.

"CAN YOU EAT GREEN
FEATHERS"

V: OLD SOMBRERO

AND how much might a parrot like this be
worth, sir?" asked Sebastian, rubbing the
yellow head of his favorite as she stood on his
shoulder reaching down for a bite of one of his
mother's tortillas.

"It would depend on the buyer," answered
the parrot peddler, turning an eye on Sebastian
as black and unwinking as the parrot's. There
was a moment's silence during which Sebastian

thought what his mother would say if she guessed he dared think of buying a useless parrot with the first money he had earned from his hard-bought pack.

"Will a parrot lay eggs for your dinner?" he could imagine her asking. "Can you eat green feathers?"

What the parrot peddler was thinking no one knows, but he said after a little:

"You understand parrots I see, my son. That's the best one I've had for years. I got her from a nest down near Chiquimula. And now I'll tell you a secret it cost me something to learn. The more yellow there is on a parrot's head the better he'll talk."

"Good polly," said Sebastian to the parrot who was cleaning her beak against his shoulder as though she had known him for years. "I have no use for a parrot myself, sir," he added to the parrot peddler, "I was just wondering." But he thought to himself that the roads would not seem lonely with a bird like that on his shoulder.

The man offered Sebastian a coarse cigarette and lit his own.

"I am a hunter," he said. "Just now I am

selling parrots. But at other times I sell other things. I hunt iguanas and alligators. Last trip I brought deer skins up to Guatemala City. And I'll tell you of something that happened to me not long ago. Are you a good Christian?"

"With God's help," said Sebastian crossing himself.

"And I too," said the man, his black eyes fixed unwinking on Sebastian, "but there are more things in the woods and mountains than the priests know about. Now I will tell you of a thing that happened to me this very year in the deer country. I had had poor luck as it happened. There were the marks of many deer, and I heard them calling at night round the village where I was staying. The moon was nearly full. Every morning when I went out I could hear them moving in the thickets. But that was as near as I came. The people of the village shook their heads.

" 'Old Sombrero is riding,' they said.

" 'Old Sombrero, and who is he, gentlemen?' I asked.

" 'Old Sombrero is Old Sombrero,' they said and shook their heads some more.

[28]

"Well, I've seen the world and am not like these ignorant people who die in the beds they were born in.

"I laughed.

"But after that I noticed that among the tracks there was one heavier than the others as though that deer carried weight. I found, too, the butts of cigarettes I had not dropped. But I am a man of the world. I laughed and thought nothing of it. Still I made up my mind I would not leave the place without a deer. I'm not accustomed to being played with."

The man stopped to light a new cigarette, and the parrot on Sebastian's shoulder pulled at his straw hat for attention. The mists swept cold and white past them, and Sebastian shivered.

"One early morning," went on the man, "I was luckier. Again with all my care the herd took flight, but this time I had a glimpse of the last of the deer. In an instant I shot at him, saw him leap into the air, and then he was off again. I had only wounded him. But he left a trail. Here a drop of blood on a leaf, there on a twig. I am a hunter and I know how to follow.

"All day I followed. I was lost but I had only

the one thought. I would not leave without a deer.

"In the late afternoon I came to a clearing in the forest with corn growing and a house in it with a hammock hanging under the porch by the door. Right into the clearing the blood led me.

" 'That's funny,' thought I.

"But there were funnier things coming. There was a hitching post outside that house and at it a couple of big deer stood, saddled and bridled. I felt something like a cold hand pass down my back. I went on. But I stood still enough when a big voice boomed 'Good evening,' at me from the hammock and Old Sombrero sat up. He was a little old man with a long white beard and a great hat on his head. I noticed he wore spurs and he was eating a big bunch of wild grapes.

" 'Have some, señor,' he said to me, and when I took them he added polite as a Christian:

" 'What may I do for you?'

"I was taken aback, but, as you know, I am a hunter.

" 'I'm following a deer, sir,' I answered, spit-

ting out the seeds. The grapes were the sweetest
I'd ever tasted.

"'And a very poor job you made of that shot,'
he said, cocking his head at me.

"I felt ashamed.

"'I had no time to aim,' I said, excusing myself, 'the devil's been in these deer.'

"He laughed.

" 'The devil has had nothing to do with it,' he said, standing up and swelling out his chest, 'they are under *my* protection.' He was not much more than four feet tall and his beard reached down to his middle.

" 'And very good protection it is,' I muttered under my breath. That pleased him. He snapped his riding whip a couple of times, lit a cigar, and finally said:

" 'Well, you might as well finish the job, sir, as let the poor brute suffer. You'll find him back in the corral. But next time remember I only allow my deer killed for actual food and I expect it done by men who know how to shoot.'

"He saw me turn red, for I'm usually a good shot and proud of it.

" 'That's all right,' he added, 'stop on your way out for a glass of beer,' and he lay down again in the hammock, keeping his feet over the edge on account of the spurs."

There was a pause long enough for Sebastian to draw one breath.

Then the man said:

"Now about this parrot. I feel drawn to you and I can see the parrot does too. I'd like you to

have her. And since it's you, you can have her
for five quetzals." A quetzal is worth a silver
dollar. The price was very high.

But Sebastian's caution was caught napping,
and his mother's opinions were forgotten. He
only thought how much he wanted this friendly
parrot and how nice it would seem to have her
company and feel her balancing on his shoulder.
Not, of course, that he was mad enough to pay
the hunter's price—he didn't have the money
in the first place. But when he started off again
up the trail, polly was perched on his shoulder
and there was not a penny in his pocket.

5 QUETZALS *for* 1 PARROT!

VI: PEDDLING

SEBASTIAN spent the night in the mountains, after all. But he and Lora, as he had named the parrot, stayed with some ox-drivers camping on a small plateau where their animals could graze. The night air was cold, and Sebastian, though curled behind a bush with Lora in his arms, woke again and again to see the great stars hung low over his head and to hear the oxen moving slowly about, chewing their cuds and quietly blowing out their breaths. At dawn he showed the men a few trinkets and managed to sell a knife and a ring, so when he started off —for oxen move slowly—he had money again in his pocket.

The road down the mountains was deserted so early in the morning. Lora and he had it to themselves. Lora squawked and flapped her wings with satisfaction. Sebastian trotted sturdily along, swinging his stick with a light

[34]

heart. The weight across his forehead did not seem so heavy now. He was thinking:

"What shall I teach Lora first?"

At last an idea came to him that made him laugh out loud. All morning he sang the same words patiently over and over to Lora, who at first remained silent, twisting her head at the sound and scrabbling with her gray claws on the wood of the cacaste where she sometimes liked to ride.

But by noon when they entered the long streets of Tecpan she had learned her part.

If Sololá had seemed like a metropolis to Sebastian, Tecpan was greater still. There were whole streets of houses with red tiled roofs, their plastered walls washed with varying colors. Even the cobbles of the roads were laid in patterns, and there was a fenced garden with a bandstand in it in front of the church. Peering through the uprights, Sebastian saw roses growing, and the trees at the corners were cut in some wonderful way to look like big baskets and chairs and animals. Along the curb a few market women had laid their produce and Sebastian sat down beyond them.

The town was quiet with the noon sun, few people passed, and no one noticed him. He and Lora amused themselves by watching the buzzards sitting on the roofs of the buildings or hopping awkwardly about the square. Big as they were, Lora was not afraid of buzzards, but she didn't like their shadows to cross over her.

They had been in their place an hour at least before Sebastian had a chance to show off Lora's new accomplishment. But he had a fine audience when it did come. A fat good-natured priest, wearing glasses, came round the corner with a young man.

"Wait a moment, your honor," said the young man as his eye lit on Sebastian's things, "let's see if there isn't something here for me to take Isabella."

The priest stopped, throwing a shadow as good as an umbrella across Sebastian. Several women loitered past and stopped too, for the priest was one of the most important men in

[36]

town. Others, seeing the knot of people, wandered up to find out what was happening.

The young man glanced at the glass jewelry and the rest of the small things, but his sweetheart was not an Indian girl to be so easily pleased. So at last the young man picked out a length of heavy yellow silk long enough for a scarf.

"Now, my lad," said he to Sebastian, "how much is this trifle worth?"

"Trifle of beaten gold!" cried Sebastian. "But you may have it for fifteen quetzals."

"Fifteen!" exclaimed the young man, drawing back as if he'd been bitten by an adder. "Fifteen, you say! Father, either this poor boy or I must be ready for a mad-house!"

"That seems dear, my son," said the fat priest to Sebastian, pursing his lips judicially.

"Dear, father?" asked Sebastian as though he couldn't believe he had heard rightly. "But it's as soft as the wings of angels! Still, since he's with your worship, I'll not be obstinate. He may have it for thirteen quetzals and I'll starve."

"That kind of starving is done on the white

meat of chickens!" said the young man venomously. "Come, father, I've been wasting your time." And he turned as though to go away, throwing the yellow silk back on the cloth.

Sebastian watched him from the corner of his eye. When he had actually taken the first step, he said mildly:

"But what, sir, is your idea of a just price?"

All were enjoying themselves greatly. The young man whirled and came back. He picked up the silk again.

"Six quetzals would be a great deal," he said, sweeping out one brown hand.

Now it was Sebastian's turn to be horrified.

"The gentleman is joking with me," he murmured, shaking his head and looking about at the circle surrounding him.

"My daughter paid more than that for her scarf, I can tell you," said one of the women sympathetically.

"Seven," exclaimed the young man, sighing deeply.

"Feel the weight, father," cried Sebastian to the priest, "it is like a banner."

[38]

"Offer the boy eight," said the priest, "though he is young to be so hard-hearted."

"Nine!" said Sebastian, and before the young man could answer he turned toward the parrot on his shoulder and asked:

"Isn't it cheap, Lora?"

Lora, hearing her cue, sang out all of a sudden in a falsetto voice:

"Ask me and I'd say
At that price it's given away!"

and burst into cackles of laughter.

But if Lora laughed hard the women laughed harder. And if the women laughed, you should have heard the priest! He slapped his leg and roared until the tears ran down behind his glasses.

"Give him his nine, Juan, and let's be off," he chuckled. "I have my prayers to say. And, my son," he added to Sebastian, "let me congratulate you on your business partner."

VII: THE SILVER ALTAR

IT HAD been a wonderful afternoon for Sebastian. He had sold more than he had ever hoped, for after Juan and the priest went away, the others who had heard Lora stayed about still laughing and bought things they had never meant to buy at all in the beginning. If the people of San Lucas Toliman could know how well he had done in the midst of these strangers, he was sure they would be proud.

Inside the great doors of the church he slipped his forehead from the leather band of his cacaste and, with Lora still on his shoulder, went respectfully into the shadowy building. On each side of him there were saints on altars bright with gildings and decorated with paintings

[40]

showing scenes from their lives. Sebastian was astonished at their beauty. At the altar rail the fat priest was kneeling alone on a prayer stool, and Sebastian knelt near him in the aisle.

But his prayers came automatically. His breath was nearly taken away by the marvels before him. Through the light of candles he could see that the whole end of the church was one huge shrine, and at its base the altar was covered with solid silver. Solid silver! He had seen silver, the little coins they handled in his village, which the women loved to pierce and string on their necklaces, but here was silver ten feet long and four feet high, and above that there was more silver, and candlesticks higher still, rimmed with cherubs' heads, and all, all of silver!

"You admire the altar, my son?" said a voice, and Sebastian looked up to see that the priest had finished his prayers and was standing above him, smiling down at him near-sightedly.

"Is it truly of silver, father?" asked Sebastian, hardly able to believe his eyes.

"Truly of silver," said the priest. "There you see hammered into the metal the figures of the four apostles and of the sun and moon. Those are shells at the corners, and the border is of roses."

"Did the angels make it?" asked Sebastian, who knew little of the wonders of the world.

"No, poor Indians like you," said the priest, smiling again, "with the help of Spanish priests like me. That was in the old days of the Conquerors when the country was still rich with gold and silver. Even the war-horses were shod with silver shoes. When this church was built—it was the second in Guatemala—Christopher Columbus's son was still alive. Look at the ceiling."

Sebastian didn't understand everything the priest said, but he didn't like to ask him questions. Obediently he looked up and saw painted beams with bosses decorated with double-headed eagles, and the faces of the new moon, and of the sun, and a bird that might have been Lora but which he guessed was a dove.

The priest pointed to the sun faces.

"Do you see the mustaches?" asked the priest. "Well, the people still say it is the face of

Alvarado, who conquered the Indians of Guatemala and took the country for the Spanish crown. His hair was so yellow that the natives called him The Sun. But he had a black heart."

Lora, tired of the smell of incense and the darkness, tweaked at Sebastian's ear.

"Come, come," said the priest who noticed everything, "she wants the sunshine, your Lora. Follow me and she shall have a lump of sugar."

Sebastian followed his broad back across a courtyard into a part of the old broken-down monastery where he had his rooms on a patio surrounded by an arcade paved with red tiles, cool behind the heavy arches that held up its roof.

In the middle of the patio was a fountain with water still brimming against its broken rim, and a table beside it on which dishes were laid to dry. Part of the ground had been made into a garden, but at the back the earth was heaped with rubbish, the arches were broken, and the evening sky showed above roofless walls.

The priest's glance followed Sebastian's.

"That is the work of old earthquakes," he said. "I might do more, but I am fat and very fond

[43]

of reading, and Maria is old." And with that he began calling loudly, "Maria! Maria! here is the boy with the parrot!"

An old Indian woman popped, like a skinny rabbit, out of one of the dark rooms. She brought them a sweet drink and then made Sebastian show her how Lora had talked in the market. How she laughed!

"I've seen many parrots in my day," she said, "but never a merchant among them until now." And she went back into her kitchen cackling like an old parrot herself.

Sebastian rose to go.

"Where will you sleep to-night?" asked the priest.

Sebastian threw out his hands and gave a little smile.

"Maria will give you a cot in the storeroom," said the other, "and there are always tortillas. We shall be glad of company. I read and hurt my eyes and have no one to whom to tell the things I read."

Never had Sebastian dreamed of such honors. He, an Indian boy, was to be the guest

[44]

of the priest of a great town like Tecpan! His
mother would die of pride if she knew.

But he remembered his manners, and bowed
his head respectfully.

"There will be dust on your honor's cloak,"
he said in a low voice, meaning that he was not
worthy of so much attention.

The fat priest peered at him good-humor-
edly.

"The favor is to me," he repeated. "I am anx-
ious for a new pair of ears. In this little place I
stifle, seeing the same faces day after day."

The priest called Tecpan a little place! Sebastian could hardly trust his hearing. Lora
gave a shrill squawk as though of derision.

"Put her in the rose bush," said the priest,
"for I have decided to tell you of that great
fighter Alvarado, and of how the Spaniards
came to these parts."

Sebastian put Lora in the nearest bush and
then squatted on his heels, his back against the
wall, where he was more comfortable than in a
chair. The priest lit a cigar.

VIII: THE CONQUERORS

"ALVARADO," began the priest, settling himself comfortably too in his big chair, "was a lieutenant of Cortez and was with him during the conquest of Mexico, that land of blood and roses. When they decided to spread the conquest south into what is now Guatemala, Cortez gave the task to Alvarado, who sent ambassadors to the Indians of these highlands.

[46]

"Your ancestors lived in many towns in houses much like yours, raising corn as you do in steep fields. They had flocks of tame turkeys and little dogs which never barked and which they used for food. They wove cloth on looms, and made pottery, hunted, and went trading as you're doing now. The women wove the same patterns into their waists that they do to-day. But the chiefs were very grand. They lived in stone houses. The stone was cut from quarries with hatchets of harder stone, and carried by men. The temples were of stone, too, built high on flights of stairs, and sometimes they offered people as sacrifices to the stone idols who sat in them. They had gardens in courtyards, with pools for water-birds, and the walls were covered with a fine whitewash on which the Spanish soldiers later used to scribble verses, criticising their leaders and asking why they didn't get their share of the loot.

"Round the towns strong walls were built as the tribes were often at war, fighting with spears and bows and arrows, and wearing for armor heavy quilts padded with cotton. The chiefs had ornamental headdresses adorned with emerald-green feathers a yard long, and their cloaks were covered with feathers, and they had gold ornaments. There were learned people, too, like me, who wrote books for learned people to read, but almost all of those have been destroyed.

"When the ambassadors came, following the Indian trade trails that ran down the backbone of Central America, they were received courteously by the chiefs. They told the Indians how mighty the Spaniards were in war, and how glorious in peace. But it was hard to make the people understand how the strangers got into the country in the first place, or how they had been able to overcome the great armies sent against them by the Aztecs of Mexico when they were so few in numbers.

"Then the ambassadors took white cloth and on it drew two pictures. The first was of a ship, with all its sails set. And the chiefs thought it a wonderful thing. They sat breathless while the interpreters explained how this was not a single log like Indian canoes, but was made from a whole forest of trees, and traveled for months like a bird, and yet could hold many men and their goods.

[48]

"The second picture was of a horse."

"A horse?" asked Sebastian, surprised.

"A horse," repeated the priest firmly, "and to the Indians of those days a very great marvel. The ambassadors told them how noble it was, shod with iron, with a cry like a trumpet, and taller than a man. They described the might of a charging war-horse riding down all who stood in its path, and yet obedient to every command of the Spaniards. Horse and rider were as one.

"And when the chiefs had seen the pictures and heard of the miraculous powers of ships and horses they decided to submit to the strangers and send them a tribute."

Sebastian couldn't help laughing. He had seen too many horses.

"The ancestors were foolish," he remarked, thinking how differently he would have acted in their places.

"You would have been like the rest," said the priest, "if you had lived when they did. *All* the Indians thought horses were gods and could not be killed, even after they saw that a horse and rider came apart. When the Aztecs at last killed one of the beasts, Montezuma had the head sent

[49]

through all Mexico to give the people courage."

"A mule is better than a horse," said Sebastian, keeping to subjects he knew about.

"It depends what it's for," said the priest. "These were very large horses. They had to be, to carry the weight of the Spaniards in their heavy armor with their silver-trimmed saddles. There could be only a few brought over each trip, and at first the chroniclers wrote down their names just as they did the soldiers'. Often two or three men owned one horse between them. And each was worth more to the generals than a dozen men.

"But if the chiefs of Guatemala, the Place of Trees, had hoped to avoid meeting these miraculous monsters, they were mistaken. They sent so much cacao, corn, cloth, gold, and jewels that it took five thousand slaves to carry it all. But so much wealth brought Alvarado quicker than ever, and with him came several hundred Spaniards, eighty horses, and some thousands of friendly Indians—friendly or terrified, that is. He treated the people of Guatemala harshly. And when a town shut its gates against him, he stormed it, with Spanish guns and steel armor

against Indian arrows and cotton quilts. He was cruel. He wished to terrify the people. Sometimes he burned the chiefs. At your lake Atitlan he drove the inhabitants of a village into the lake, but they swam to an island and escaped in the night."

"I know the place," said Sebastian.

"When there was not a chief left who dared raise his head without permission," the priest went on, closing his eyes and talking in his great voice like a big bee booming in a hollyhock flower, "Alvarado built a town in a fine valley at the foot of the volcano of Agua or Hunapu as it was called then. He named it The City of the Gentlemen of Saint James of Guatemala. He was its governor, and to crown his pride he went back to Spain and married a great lady, Doña Beatrice de la Cueva, and brought her home to his palace in Guatemala. In her train came twenty gentlewomen of noble birth and many negro slaves, both men and women, and her passing was like a queen's."

Sebastian was not at all sure what a queen was, but he felt he had interrupted enough.

"But before many years had gone by," the

[51]

priest said with apparent satisfaction, "Alvarado was killed in Mexico by the fall of one of
these victory-winning horses. When word of his
death reached Lady Beatrice she was mad

with grief. She drove anyone away who tried
to comfort her and hung all the palace with
black. When she had to sign papers of state, she
wrote The Unfortunate One, instead of her

name. A month crawled by. And then a terrible thing happened. For days the rain fell, more like a river pouring out of heaven than rain, and the earth shook so that a man could hardly stand. At last the quakes grew so fierce that the tiles were thrown from the roofs like autumn leaves in a gale, and the dogs ran in terror howling through the streets, and the bells of the churches rang by themselves as though they were tolling for the death of the city.

"Then the terrified inhabitants heard a rending sound above them as though the mountain were breaking in two, and the lake, which lay in Hunapu's crater, was seen pouring down the slope carrying an avalanche with it. Lady Beatrice and her companions ran through the palace and up the steep stairs that led to a tower on the roof. But even that was not high enough to save them. The water followed them and they were drowned, and the few citizens who escaped from the disaster whispered that the flood had come as a punishment upon Lady Beatrice for refusing comfort when her husband died."

The fat priest paused and thought to himself, his eyes on the ruins at the back of his garden.

"But others," he went on after a little, "say it was a judgment on all the Spaniards because of their cruelty to the Indians whom they had enslaved and used as beasts of burden. The priests did what they could, but it was not much. Men were starved to death and worked to death and killed outright in spite of their protests. So, some say, Hunapu, the great volcano, took matters into its own hands to punish the destruction of its people. Afterwards the priests christened it with a new name and called it Agua, or water, and blessed it and the other volcanoes, too, hoping to tame them. More Spaniards came and they built a larger city which is now called Antigua."

"However," the fat priest added, "the volcanoes are not yet reconciled. Whatever they want they still grumble and rock the ground and now and then knock down cities."

But Sebastian was no longer listening. His face had turned white.

"Lora!" he called horrified. Lora, who had been very quiet, cocked her head wickedly. There was hardly a rose left on the bush. They all lay in a circle on the ground beneath her, each stem cleanly cut by the strong scissors of her beak.

"Oh, Lora! Lora!" cried Sebastian ready to cry with vexation. What *would* the good priest think! But the priest was laughing again.

"Let her alone, my son," said he. "Isn't she a lady parrot? She has a right to a few flowers."

And he was still laughing when Maria called them to eat a fine dinner at a table she had set farther down the arcade.

IX: THE GIANTS

THE first daylight was filtering into the storeroom when Sebastian woke quietly. His cot had seemed very soft to him with its canvas spread smoothly between stretchers. He was used to the ground or a hard bed of rawhide woven like wire netting and covered with a thin grass mat. His first glance was for Lora. There she was at the edge of the cot, her head still under her wing.

Then he almost screamed. For over him he saw a face with fierce yellow mustaches, and then a staring lady's face, and beside them two negroes with rolling eyes. They were all much bigger than life and at least eight feet from the floor, and he could see four huge dangling pink

[56]

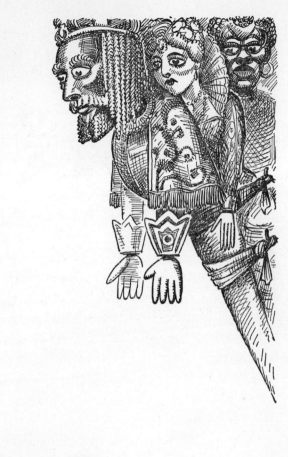

Great staring faces.

hands, but the negroes' hands seemed worse, for in the shadows he couldn't see them at all.

"Oh, Lora! Lora!" he whimpered. "It's Alvarado!" And he covered his head with his blanket and waited to feel the clutch of one of those pink hands on his shoulder. But after a while, when nothing happened, he remembered that he was almost a man now, and stole another look at the ogres. They had not moved. Their round cheeks shone and their eyes stared over his head. Now he could see that they had no bodies, but were only dummies built on frameworks. How he had fooled himself! But even now such neighbors gave him the creeps. He stole out of bed, still keeping his eyes warily on them, and backed out of the door into the courtyard. He felt safer on the rim of the fountain teaching Lora something new. She was quick to learn but he wasn't sure she was perfect when the priest's servant came to lay the table for breakfast.

What fine living there was at the father's house! Hot tortillas wrapped in a red napkin, black beans, baked plantains, and coffee with hot milk! When everything was ready, Maria called the priest who came out of his room, smiling and polishing his glasses.

"Well, how did you peddlers sleep?" he asked after he had wished them all good morning.

"The bed was like silk," answered Sebastian. The father gave him a quick look.

"You say so much but no more. Now what was wrong, my son?"

"I was afraid of Alvarado and the Lady Beatrice and her ladyship's two black slaves," said Sebastian in a burst.

"Alvarado and the Lady Beatrice and her ladyship's two black slaves?" repeated the priest, staring.

"The boy means the Corpus Christi giants surely, your honor," said old Maria, cackling. "They're kept in the storeroom and, now I think of it, they were near where I put the cot last night."

"The Corpus Christi giants," said the priest and laughed until he almost lost his breath.

"Oh, Sebastian," he exclaimed when he could speak again, "you must stay with us a week! Haven't you giants in San Lucas Toliman? Here Corpus Christi couldn't go on if the

[60]

giants didn't lead the procession. Maria dresses them up in all sorts of old curtains and odds and ends, and the biggest boys walk inside them. Did I say walk? They dance and whirl and the giants' hands fly out like windmills. They're rough, our giants! And so you thought Alvarado would fly off with you through the roof, did you?"

"To a country toad a blade of grass seems a cypress," murmured Sebastian, taking a bite of tortilla and nearly choking with shame. He had felt such a man in the market only the afternoon before!

"But perhaps you're right," said the priest, turning sober again. "Perhaps it is in memory of Alvarado that the giants were first made here. It's an idea I must think over," and he asked Maria for more coffee.

Sebastian felt happier. The good father was going to think over something he, Sebastian, had said! Well, well. And with all his duties he seemed in no hurry to leave the table. He even gave Lora milk in a silver spoon, which she drank eagerly, working her hard bill and black rubber tongue in sipping it up.

[61]

But at last it was time for Sebastian to be off, for he must shoulder his wonderful pack. He kissed the priest's hand and thanked him for his kindness from the bottom of his heart. Then he said:

"And what do you say, Lora?"

What Lora said was nothing at all.

"And what do you say, Lora?" asked Sebastian again louder, feeling foolish.

Again Lora said nothing at all.

But when she was on his shoulder and they were leaving the patio, she suddenly changed her mind and, spreading her wings, broke out calling at the top of her lungs until even Maria ran out of her kitchen:

"May your reward
Come from the Lord!"

So, after all, the last sight Sebastian had of the good priest was of his mouth open in a wide laugh beneath the twin circles of his glasses, and the last sound he heard was a sound of good-natured chucklings.

X: PLEASANT DAYS

BEYOND Tecpan the mountains spread their folds into valleys, and the towns bordered the road like big beads tied on a brown string. Sebastian traded in all of them and did well with the help of Lora. If people looked at his wares but hung back from buying he'd say:

"What shall we do, Lora?"

And Lora would scream out, flapping her wings:

"Trade's slow!

Let's go!"

How people laughed! So, with one thing and another, the pack grew lighter, Sebastian's shoulders grew stronger, and the road always led downhill.

They were fine days. He liked to pass the women washing clothes at the fountains outside the villages, all talking together and hanging their wash on the bushes to dry. They called out to Sebastian as he passed, and both he and Lora answered them politely, "Adios," which means "Be With God." Sometimes he stopped, showing them his things. Once a man rode by with silver work across the back of the cantle of his saddle, and Sebastian thought of Alvarado and his horses. In one large town the Spanish fountain in the plaza was carved with stone parrots as big as a boy, and the water fell from their weather-stained beaks. Sebastian tried to point them out to Lora, but Lora refused to recognize them and sidled impatiently up and down his shoulder, chattering to herself in her own parrot language.

Sometimes the flat plains suddenly gaped into narrow ravines down which their road led, with a stream to keep them company. In one of these there was a fine mill with courtyards and wagon sheds and mill buildings and a long dormitory where the men slept, with a chapel in the

[64]

middle. Its name was The Mountain Mill. Sebastian wandered through its gate in hope of trade. Everyone seemed too busy to buy anything, but he was allowed to go where he pleased, and so it happened that he found the great serpent's head on the hillside. It was carved from a single block of stone and there was a man's head between its open jaws.

He squatted down on his heels in front of it. Something told him it was the work of The Ancestors, of the Indians of old times, and a feeling almost of fear rose in his heart as he looked into the great stone eyes of the snake. He was so intent that he didn't hear the footsteps that stopped beside him, and jumped when a voice said:

"Well, what do you make of our snake—a big one, eh?"

Sebastian got quickly to his feet. It was a white man, and he knew there were many in the country, men from a place called Germany who raised coffee, and men from the North who went by the name of Americans and laid down roads of steel called railroads and raised millions of bananas along the coast with the aid of black men from the islands. But except for the Spanish priests he had never spoken with a white man before. Respectfully he pulled off his straw hat.

"Tell me, sir," he asked eagerly, "what is it for?"

"It's for nothing now," said the man, "but I suppose it was the end of a temple balustrade once. Indian of course. I've seen cities buried in the jungle with stone kings in headdresses of feathers, each one with an altar in front of him. There were pyramids more than a hundred

feet high, over-
grown with
trees, with the
ruins of courts
and temples on
the top, and all the
steps pushed out of
place by roots and saplings.
The balustrades were big snakes
ending in heads like this. If you look close you
can see bits of the red and green paint left, although it's probably a thousand years old."

Sebastian dropped back to his heels and from
there he could see the red paint still clinging in
the corners of the flat jaws and the blind eyes. In
a surge there swept over him a sense of the might
of a serpent, of the long legless body strong and
supple, the flat head shaped like a spear thrust-
ing its way along the ground, the cold staring
eyes, and the horny mouth drawing back to show
the flickering tongue.

Lora pulled at his straw hat and Sebastian
came to himself with a start and unconsciously
crossed himself. The white man was looking at
him curiously.

[67]

"So they still feel it," he said to himself.

Sebastian took his leave a little dazed.

"With God," he said soberly.

"With God," said the man.

And Sebastian trotted back to the road and once more went on his way, and soon forgot the stone snake and the queer excitement he had felt.

About four o'clock he came to a flat place among the hills where an ox-cart was already drawn up at the side of the road, the animals grazing and the driver amusing himself by playing on a mouth organ.

"How far is it to Antigua, sir?" asked Sebastian.

"Three hours for me and two hours for you," said the man, "but are you in a hurry?"

"No," said Sebastian.

"Are those fair things you have in your ca-caste?" asked the man.

"Yes," said Sebastian.

"Then I advise you," said the ox-driver, who seemed to be one of those people who like to make plans for others, "to spend the night here, and stop in the morning at San Felipe just outside Antigua. For the pilgrims are gathering there and the booths, they tell me, are set up already."

"What is the pilgrimage?" asked Sebastian.

"Is it possible you've never heard of the Black Christ who lies there in a casket of glass?" exclaimed the man, opening his eyes wide. "Why, more miracles are performed there than at any church for a hundred miles."

"A cock knows only the affairs of his own barnyard," said Sebastian, "it's the first time I've ever taken the road."

The man played a tune on his mouth organ, and the noise set Lora to whistling with all her might. Her tune was different but just as loud, and when she grew tired of it, she laughed until they both laughed with her.

"Look here," said the ox-driver when he had finished. "You're hot and tired and dusty. Now right up that trail a mile you'll find the hot springs of San Lorenzo. For a trifle you can bathe there and you'll feel like a new man. I'll keep your pack for you."

The idea seemed good to Sebastian—all except the part about leaving his pack behind.

"How warm is the water?" he asked.

"Warm as a summer's day to a person," said the driver, "but it will boil an egg in five minutes on the sand. You can sit on the steps and peel an egg out of the shell after your bath."

"You can't unless you have an egg," said Sebastian regretfully.

"I'll give you one," said the man, and he went to the back of his wagon and in a moment brought one back.

"Be very careful not to break it," he said, serious as an owl, but as Sebastian, Lora, and the pack started off up the valley, they heard him playing again merrily.

Sebastian carried the precious egg very carefully indeed, and after a short mile they came to the end of the little valley they had been following. A pink wall had been built across the head of the stream and a small adobe house for dressing in. Two women were washing clothes in the warm water which flowed through a hole in the wall. A ragged boy came down from the side of a hill to collect three cents from Sebastian, who then went into the house, locked the door by propping a stick against one of its panels and, slipping off his clothes, hurried down some mossy steps into the open pool, which lay clear as glass under a little cliff hung with ferns.

Oh, what a joy it was to feel the soft warm water flowing about one! It came almost to his shoulders. Looking down he could see hundreds of bubbles rising through the sand, and he himself was outlined with a band of bright green and blue, which widened or narrowed as he moved. Very carefully he laid the egg in a shallow place where he could reach it again, while Lora stood on one of the steps and scolded as he splashed.

It was not five minutes but twenty before he finally dragged himself away, first carefully getting the egg which seemed only a little warm.

"That can't be boiled!" thought Sebastian, but when he broke it open, sure enough it was hard all through, and Lora and he ate it with much satisfaction. Here was another story to tell the stay-at-homes in San Lucas Toliman, who had never heard of a spring no warmer than a dog's tongue, which yet would boil an egg!

But somehow that was one story Sebastian never told. For that evening when he was eating his supper with the ox-driver, the man brought a basket from the back of his cart.

"Have a San Lorenzo egg!" he said and went off into guffaws of laughter. For his wife had boiled him a dozen so that they wouldn't be broken when the cart went into a chuck-hole.

Still, thought Sebastian, if the ox-driver had his joke, he, Sebastian, had two good eggs out of it.

XI: THE LAME MAN

THE road leading to San Felipe and Antigua was crowded as roads go. There were
country women in gay clothes going to town,
their heavy loads in baskets on their heads. There
were pilgrims, too, who had already walked
miles since dawn, carrying with them what they
needed while away, the mothers with babies on
their backs, and the fathers often carrying a
little child or two on the top of their cacastes.
Sebastian noticed they had candles with them
wrapped in banana leaves to protect them from
the sun, with a flower or two stuck in the folds.

It was too early for the ox-carts to be far on
their way, but once he heard hoofs behind him
and got out of the road while three women, sit-

ting awkwardly sideways in saddles like chairs, rode by on runtish horses. One woman carried an umbrella, and Sebastian watched it bobbing up and down until they were out of sight.

For the first time Sebastian began to pass the coffee fincas or plantations, like cool green woods, with protecting trees planted in rows, under which the coffee bushes with their shiny leaves grew like some wonderful underbrush. Most of the fincas were large and owned by rich men from the capital, or foreigners, often Germans. Each had a small village of its own, but the Indians in them were all in debt to their masters and couldn't leave. If they ran away, soldiers were sent after them to bring them back. Sebastian had known men from San Lucas Toliman who had needed money and had gone to work on the fincas. Sometimes they were allowed to return for a little while in spring to plant their own cornfields. Then they said the life was a good one, food for all, a roof for a

[74]

man's head, and medicine if he was sick. But when they were drunk they cried and said they were slaves and that even their children were sold to the finqueros.

Sebastian with his pack on his back, Lora on his shoulder, and the right to follow any path he wanted to, felt sorry for the workers on the fincas who could not even go to near-by San Felipe as he was going. It had not rained for months and the volcanic dust of the road rose in little spurts under his sandals at every step. He felt happy and friendly toward all the world.

Yet he didn't like the lame man who joined him, hobbling along at his side and watching him like a lizard from small black eyes, while he asked him questions: where was he going? where had he come from? what was in his pack? had he sold many things?

Sebastian answered more and more shortly and walked faster and faster. The sweat dripped under the band of his cacaste, but still the lame man kept at his side. He was carrying a machete in a leather scabbard at his belt, a knife a foot and a half long, which the Indians use in their work and also for fighting. There was something sly and fierce about him and he had been drinking aguardiente, or white eye, as the people call it. When, on a lonely stretch of road between villages, he stopped and asked Sebastian to open his pack, the boy felt his heart beginning to beat hard against his ribs.

But he kept on walking.

"I'm in a hurry to get to San Felipe," he said in a voice he tried to keep from shaking, "you can see everything there, friend."

The lame man started to say something, but by luck they turned a corner and came full on a cantina or roadside drinking house with several people clustered at the door.

"Until later," the man called in an ugly voice and limped off to drink again. Sebastian was glad to be rid of him. Once in the crowd at San Felipe he hoped they wouldn't meet. More than once he had seen men slashed by machetes and it was a terrible sight.

He passed a village with a large church, pink

as the inside of a watermelon, beside a square filled with purple-blossoming trees. There was also a bandstand, where on Sunday evenings the village band would play while the girls walked one way round the square and the men strolled in the opposite direction. From there he followed the pilgrims down a deeply worn lane and found himself beside San Felipe. There was only a church, no village, but booths had been set up round it, and families were camped along its walls, their bundles hanging from orange trees and their little cooking fires sending up narrow ribbons of smoke among the spires.

The pilgrims wore garlands of long pepper leaves about their hats, and the booths were filled with San Felipe rosaries, strings of hard candies wrapped in bits of corn husk dried and dyed in the brightest colors. The people bought them and wore them about their necks or across their shoulders. There were sellers of real rosaries, too, and of holy pictures and small baskets and little wooden boxes painted with flowers. Sebastian noticed several eating booths and stands covered with glasses of colored pop thickened with corn meal or grated cocoanut, and there

[77]

was one tent with paintings of a blue-eyed snake woman changed to so horrid a shape because of her sins.

Before opening his pack, Sebastian went into the church. At the entrance were small paintings put there by people who had prayed to the Christ of San Felipe in the midst of some danger and believed it was that prayer which had saved them. The pictures were very exciting, and badly drawn, and showed men falling from windmills, and women on the horns of bulls, and operations, and charging railroad engines, and boats sinking, and runaway horses, and other dangerous scenes as well.

Sebastian looked at them one by one, and then put off his pack and went to pray where a whole bank of candles lit up the long curls of real hair and the beautiful dark face and hands of the Black Christ who lay in robes of lace in a glass casket, just as the ox-driver had described him. All round Sebastian other Indians were kneeling, holding candles. The hot wax dripped over their hands but they never noticed. Their packs stood against the walls, their babies played about their knees, and a little white dog ran in from the street but no one paid any attention. Sometimes a whole family shared a big candle. The father would hold it first, his lips moving in prayer, then he would hand it to his wife, and later she would let the older children have their turn. But sometimes the man had come alone, perhaps all the way from Mexico, and then he held half a dozen candles in his hands, one for each one of his family he had left behind.

Sebastian went out to one of the booths and bought a candle too. Then he prayed for his mother and all the people of San Lucas Toliman and for himself and for Lora who sat quietly on his shoulder. When he had finished he set his candle to burn with others on the great stand in front of the altar and went out into the square.

There Lora found her tongue. All day Sebastian sold things. People were in a buying mood. Everyone wanted something to take home from their pilgrimage, and the boy with the parrot always had a crowd about him.

Once he thought he saw the lame man among the people, but he wasn't sure, and by this time he had almost forgotten him. But by late afternoon the crowd had thinned, and Sebastian de-

cided to see Antigua before it grew dark. With
his lightened pack again on his back, he started
out.

When he had walked a short distance he came
to a blind man sitting by the side of the road,
begging for alms. A little dog sat beside him

with a cocked tail and merry beady eyes.
The dog was on a leading string and looked
as though he knew how to take care of
his master. A woman ahead of Sebastian
stopped, took the load off her head, felt in a
cloth and took out three tortillas which she

placed carefully in the blind man's groping hands.

Sebastian thought how his mother had said, "Remember your prayers." Charity was a kind of prayer, he knew, and so he gave the blind man a little silver coin.

"God bless you," said the blind man.

"With God," answered Lora promptly.

"Is that a parrot?" asked the blind man. "Are you the boy with the parrot?"

"Yes," said Sebastian, proud that a stranger should have heard about them.

"Then you must look out," went on the beggar. "Not long ago a lame man passed this way. I could hear one step heavy and one step light. He was boasting that if he met you he would slit your pack with his machete—have you a pack?"

"Yes," said Sebastian.

"And he said he would slit you too," the blind man went on. "He was drunk. He said you wouldn't show him your things. There was something else he said but I forget."

"A thousand thanks," said Sebastian, shivering as though a cold wind had suddenly struck

[81]

him. "If I see him I'll take to my heels." And he left the blind man with the bright-eyed little dog in their place beside the road.

But before they were quite out of hearing the blind man remembered what it was he hadn't been able to think of before. "And he said he'd twist your parrot's neck too!" he called after them in a voice far-off and quavering.

But in spite of the blind man's warning, Sebastian enjoyed seeing Antigua. The Spaniards had built it hundreds of years ago after the Lady Beatrice was drowned in her tower, but the earthquakes had found them out. Sixty great churches and convents they built with bells in their towers and the Volcano of Fire had

[82]

knocked them down and shaken the belfries as a
boy shakes a cherry tree. So once more the people
moved away, this time to the Valley of Cows,
and built the new city of Guatemala, leaving
Antigua, the old city, behind them with only the
fronts of the great churches standing and the
painted saints in their niches blessing the empty
streets. For ten years the carriers had trotted to
and fro on the mountainous road carrying household goods from the old city to the new, but
there were some people who would not leave.
They put up new beams across old walls and
covered them with unbroken tiles, and planted
their gardens again, and repaired a few of the
churches. These things took place more than a
hundred years ago in the old days before Guatemala threw off the government of Spain and
became a republic. But the city had not changed.

Sebastian saw its low houses painted all the

colors of the rainbow, and at almost every corner he found the high façade of a beautiful church with the sky showing through its cracks and goats and donkeys grazing in its broken patios. The great market was held in a ruined monastery; blacksmiths and weavers worked in rooms where abbots had once lived; angels without hands looked at Sebastian smiling; cracked bells which had not rung for a hundred and fifty years still hung like bats from their heavy beams in the towers; and buzzards perched where the Spanish coat-of-arms of another time showed the lions of Leon and the castles of Castile.

Most of this Sebastian understood from the talk he had heard. He looked at everything, peered through the open doorways into courtyards green with ferns and palms; noticed the electric lights hanging in the houses; hurried up on the narrow sidewalks to make room for a passing carriage or a rare automobile; and admired the fine town women in their wide flounced skirts and bright silk scarves, whose feet, however, were often bare like his mother's.

He didn't feel out of place among these people who were half of his blood and half Spanish.

[84]

There were many Indians about him, too, each dressed in the fashion of his or her village. They trickled like a constant stream through the streets of the city, and the inhabitants sat in their doorways, like smooth pebbles along a bank, watching the others go by. While Sebastian was wandering aimlessly, looking at everything, he was suddenly surprised to feel the ground tremble under his feet and to hear the small bronze hands on the doors begin knocking gently against the wood.

It was an earthquake, not by any means the first he had felt in that land of volcanoes. He braced his feet and the earth seemed to move under him in long waves of solid substance. Lora screamed, and on every side they saw people run out of the houses into the middle of the streets. The windows rattled loudly in their frames, the earth rose and subsided more violently under Sebastian's feet, and then it was all over. Everyone laughed and went back to their houses. They had not been at all frightened. It was an everyday occurrence. But no one could tell beforehand how strong a shock might become and they knew the danger from the heavy tiles of their roofs.

Sebastian, laughing too, walked on. Soon he came to the square where the old palace stretched its block of double pillars, and the cathedral raised its patched ruins above a garden of dusty flowers and small modern statues. In the evening light the tall cones of the volcanoes of Fire and Water seemed thin as a veil and purple as violets high above the town. Smoke was rising from their sides where men were clearing the land during the last of the dry season for corn, just as they did on the rocky slopes of his own Atitlan. The same mountains overlooked San Lucas Toliman.

His thoughts went to his mother's land and he was filled with the memory of young green shoots forcing their way up among the black stones of old lava flows. A wave of homesickness came over him, not for his mother or his village, but for the sound of the first rain and the sight of the new corn. It was that way with all Indians. They had tamed the corn and it was their life. Red civilizations had risen and fallen following the corn. He did not know it but a

[86]

thousand years ago his remote ancestors in the lowlands had carved on their monuments young gods climbing among the tassels of the stalks. Now at Easter time the mountain villages marked the path of the saints from the church to the well by a row of green corn stalks brought from far off. The fire on the mountains was a symbol of preparation. It was more holy to him than the candles on an altar, although he could not have found words for his feeling.

This year a neighbor would clear their ground but he must be back to plant it. He lifted his pack. It was more than half empty but it was too heavy. He felt the tug of his own patch of soil, of the waiting seed. He looked about. It was too late to sell anything now. Lora pulled at his hat, and for the first time he spoke to her impatiently.

Sebastian had forgotten all about the lame man as he walked back toward San Felipe, but the lame man had not forgotten about him. The road was lonely, and suddenly he heard the sound of feet running behind him and with a chill he realized that the gait was uneven. He glanced over his shoulder and then started off

[87]

like a rabbit, Lora hanging on for dear life. He had seen the glint of light along the man's machete, and even in that quick glance he could see how fast he was coming. Sebastian's pack bumped against him as he ran. He thought of dropping it off but anything seemed better than abandoning his fortune.

Behind him he could hear the unsteady feet drawing closer, he could catch the deep breathing of the runner. With a spurt of speed he turned a corner and dodged into an open doorway and through a dark room into a court beyond. Weak all over, he leaned against the wall, panting and listening. Close behind he heard the pursuing feet turn the corner and rush past, and then someone whom he had not seen in the room quietly closed the heavy door to the street and barred it.

He dodged into an open doorway.

XII: THE WHISTLES

IT DID not take the lame man long to guess that Sebastian had taken to cover somewhere near. Soon a great pounding and hammering began on the door that someone had closed. Suppose the people of the house opened to see who was knocking! But just then out of the darkness of the room through which Sebastian had run, came a small thin man, in a sort of apron spotted with paint.

He gave Sebastian a somewhat toothless smile. "Let him knock, it will help to sober him," he said, turning his back on the uproar at his door which continued furiously for some minutes and then at last died away. But as the noise at the door subsided, another rose louder

still in the courtyard where the daylight lin-
gered. The place seemed full of parrots. Like
most poor houses there was only one real room,
the long narrow one through which Sebastian
had run, where the family beds stood and the
little images of the household saints in glass cases
on a bureau. A porch stretched along the back of
the house facing the courtyard, and here the
family lived during the daytime, eating their
meals and working. To one side was the kitchen,
sooty as a blacksmith's shop, with an oven instead of a forge, and the red light of pine knots
flickering on its walls. Here as usual a woman
was grinding corn into fine meal on a stone and
then mixing it with water and patting it into tortillas to brown.

There was a well in the courtyard, an unused
shed for mules, several fruit trees, and a pile of
wood for the kitchen. On this pile stood the first
parrot screaming, sidling up and down a log,
while a second parrot, hanging on a stick between the uprights of the porch, screamed in
chorus and gritted his beak. A little white curly
dog ran out from under a table and added his
high yapping to the din, and a thin yellow cat

which had been sleeping in a basket near a brown dove, woke, blinked its eyes, and stretched sleepily.

To add to the noise several children appeared from nowhere and shouted at the parrots, and the woman laughed.

All this was on account of Lora. The sight of a strange parrot threw the other birds into a fury. They ruffled their feathers as a watchdog raises the hair on his spine, and Lora, taking a firm grip on Sebastian's shoulder—"ouch!" said he—squawked back her defiance.

But at last peace was restored, and Sebastian gratefully accepted the invitation of the master of the house to spend the night there.

"It is wiser," said the man. "The lame fool is probably harmless in himself. But to-night the whisky sings wickedly in him, and his machete knows the tune."

Sebastian had been looking in the dusk at the long tables that ran down the porch. They were covered with small clay animals, some no bigger than the tip of your finger, pigs, dogs, sheep, goggle-eyed frogs, swans, and owls. On one table he could make out that the creatures were of rough clay, but on the next table they were bright with paint. Along the back stood rows of owls and swans, some of them a foot high. The larger ones were banks and the smaller ones were whistles or toys.

Sebastian picked up a yellow owl whistle and blew a shrill hoot that set Lora squawking again. But just then the man lit a candle, and she saw one of the big owls and retreated close against her master's cheek, trembling.

"Ah, she knows it's an owl!" cried the little man much pleased. "See! it's not every day I get such a compliment." And he called Lora a clever bird and tried to stroke her head, but she bit him.

"Excuse her, sir," said Sebastian, "she is still nervous because of the owls."

The man was used to parrots.

"Sit down," he said, lighting another candle and picking up his brushes. "I am working late so that these may dry off for the San Felipe fair. I am a little behindhand. I've not been well. These are some of the famous Antigua animals that are our specialty here."

"May I try?" asked Sebastian after he had

[94]

watched for a while. The man gave him a rather stubbly brush and he began with easy ones like a white pig with a black spot or two and a red speck at the end of its snout. But while he painted one, the toymaker did five.

Next he tried an owl, breathing hard and biting his lip. But the owls were harder. There were feathers and claws and white touched into each eye to make it look shiny. Sebastian's owl had the air of having been out in a wind, but the thin man pretended there was nothing wrong about it, and Sebastian thought it was wonderful.

"I'd like to make lots of kinds," he said, spreading out his brown hands, "parrots and policemen and carriers and women with baskets. And I'd make each whistle sound different to fit."

The thin man coughed and put down his work to stare at Sebastian.

"Where'd you get that idea?" he demanded.

"I just made it up, sir," said Sebastian, surprised.

The toymaker went into the house and brought back something which he laid very carefully in Sebastian's hands. It was the head of a wild goose done in unpainted clay.

"Blow it," he said.

Sebastian blew and from his mouth sounded the cry of a flying goose, a solitary lonesome sound which set the parrots screaming.

"I'm a maker of whistles," said the man, "and my father was before me, and his father was before that, so I'm naturally interested in whistles. Two years ago a man came through here carrying a pack like yours, mostly full of such things as yours, but he had with him a few of these clay whistles, more as curiosities than to sell. He came from Yucatan near the old cities, and they find these in the fields. He had one with two mouths that blew at once, like the call of a hawk, and another one that had seven mouths and would play a whole scale. This was the only one he would sell, but he had some with funny figures on them, prisoners and kings, and one was a woman with a dog under one arm, holding a child by the hand. I happened to see them like this, by candle-light. They seemed ready to move and I said to myself, 'Here are the Ancestors, but grown very small, and with whistles for voices.'"

The woman came up.

"You'll have a whistle for a voice yourself if you don't get something to eat soon," she said, laughing. "And will you bless our table by eating with us?" she added to Sebastian.

So once more he sat down with strangers, and ate, watched by the eyes of a whole row of yellow clay owls, while somewhere outside the lame man stumbled from cantina to cantina, drinking and feeling the edge of his machete and muttering about the boy with the parrot who wouldn't open his pack.

XIII: THE ROAD TURNS

BUT the lame man either landed in jail that night or went home to work and sobriety. Sebastian and Lora saw him no more though they stayed at San Felipe for three whole days until they had sold everything but a roll of red ribbon which Sebastian put aside for the toy-maker's wife. She was greatly pleased with it, but she refused to take money from him.

"What is a roof," she asked, "and a corner of the children's bed? Do you harm us? As for the food, God be praised, we still have enough for our friends. Would we feed Chico here," and she patted the white dog, "if we had to turn Christians from our door?"

Sebastian left the cacaste in a corner of their porch out of the way, and with a pocket full of money, and Lora on his shoulder, walked the thirty miles to Guatemala City to see the capital. But he was now used to marvels. He stared calmly at the market though it would have held all San Lucas Toliman under its broad roofs. He took Lora for an exciting ride on the city's one street car that pitched like a hard-gaited horse. He saw a dozen automobiles at once and stores whose windows were filled with images, not of saints, but of ladies and gentlemen in foreign clothes. But over the roofs he saw the outlines of Agua and the faint smoke of far-off fires. He could almost imagine green corn sprouting between the diamond-shaped paving stones. And clouds were beginning to gather over the highlands. He smelled the air and watched the birds flying to guess how soon the rains would come.

Nevertheless in the city there was one window which held him spellbound. Again and again he returned to it, and stood leaning against the glass, staring in. He had heard of such things, but he had not seen one before. There was a lady in white who showed how it should be used. He never grew tired watching her while Lora pulled at his hat unnoticed. At first she had pecked at her reflection in the glass but that didn't amuse her for more than a minute and now she longed for motion and new sights. She was a born gadabout.

But Sebastian was glued to the window. Not for a long time did it occur to him that his pocket was full of money and that he could buy the thing he admired. Its price was on a placard. Yes, he had all that and more. There would be enough left over to buy another pack when the corn had been harvested. He and his mother were so poor they needed no money. If they bought land they would have more than they could work. A cow was much trouble and they weren't used to milk. His mother made all their clothes herself on a loom at the back of the house, and as to the house he never thought of changing it. It had always been small and dark, but it was large enough for two and it kept out the rain. It would do no more if it were sky blue and had windows with bars of iron.

For himself he had already bought a new straw hat which he put on top of the old one to carry home safely. He had wanted Lora and there she was on his shoulder. Now in all the great city the one thing he yearned for was behind the glass window.

It was better than the finest toy, with its big wheels and little wheels. And then how pleasantly it would sound when his mother used it in the evenings! All San Lucas Toliman would come to wonder and admire. How it would save his mother, and she could earn money with it, too, if she wished.

So at last he reminded himself that there is no landslide without a slipping pebble, and got himself into the great neat shop, both hats in his hand, so awed he could hardly speak above a whisper.

But somehow the great purchase was made. Half an hour later Sebastian came out of the store, his hats once more on his head, Lora on his shoulder, his pockets far emptier than they'd been, and an enormous load on his back. It bowed him down as the pack had never done. He had to lean far forward and help himself

[101]

with his stick. And the road before him wound upward over the mountains for more than a hundred miles.

But his heart was almost bursting with joy and pride. He and Lora were returning to San Lucas Toliman in triumph from their adventure. Above him he saw the clouds slowly forming in long dark banners and he heard a roll of thunder without lightning. The rains were drawing near, but it would take them days before they locked horns with the drought. He would be home in time for the planting.

Mile by mile he left the city behind him. He did not regret it. He was returning home crowned with success. For he had not forgotten his mother's final words to him. He had remembered his manners and his prayers, and now his back was a witness that he remembered his mother too.

"A sewing machine from the North all for her own. She will be proud as the sun on Easter day!" Sebastian boasted to Lora as they climbed, and Lora stood on his shoulder, flapped her wings, and squawked for joy at being on the road once more.